Ravenhill Court

David R. Beshears

Based on the screenplay
"Ravenhill Court"

Greybeard Publishing
Washington State

ISBN 978-0-9914327-0-7 *(print edition)*

Greybeard Publishing
P.O. Box 480
McCleary, WA 98557-0480

Ravenhill Court

Prolog

Present Day

Ben Foster drove the fifties era Mercury slowly across the Edgewood Street intersection and into Ravenhill Court. He turned into the driveway of the second house on the right and stopped. Turning off the engine, he took a few moments to look out at the old neighborhood.

There were nine houses on the dead-end cul-de-sac, nestled into the grassy California foothills. They had once been comfortable, middleclass homes. They were now fifty years old and long abandoned. Lawns were overgrown and yellowed. Some of the doors stood open; a curtain fluttered through an open window; a rain gutter had pulled away from an eave; a screen door, bent and torn, slapped against its jam in the slight breeze.

He opened the door and climbed out of the car. The quiet felt heavy. There was the sound of the breeze brushing past his ears, and the sound of the screen door across the street, and nothing else. No other sounds at all; not from the other houses, not from the surrounding hills, and no sound reached into Ravenhill Court from the outside. It was as if this street and its collection of houses were all that existed. There was no outside world.

Ben Foster, middle-aged, hair slightly graying, a job in the city, hadn't been in Ravenhill in forty years or more. He wasn't sure why, but for some strange reason he wasn't able to pin down exactly when he had left. And it hadn't just been him... everyone had left.

He turned his attention back to the trunk of the car. Reaching in, he brought out a large, leather-bound book. With the journal in hand, he walked down to the sidewalk and stood at the curb. Another strange sensation, as if the past was reaching out across the years and touching him on the shoulder. He looked at the house across the street; at Peter's house.

Mrs. Murray called out to him; a distant, far-away voice. "Ben? Ben... where's Peter?"

Ben Foster sat down on the curb and rested the journal in his lap. He rubbed his hand across the leather cover. He heard a child's voice then. His voice.

"Hey, Mrs. Murray. He had to stay after."

Peter had to stay after. Ben's skin felt as though he had walked into a spider's web. He fought the urge to wipe his face. He looked down at the journal, stirred up the courage and finally opened it. The pages were yellowed. On the first page was written *The Ravenhill Journals.* The words had been carefully written, as if the young author had been very serious about what he was starting. There was something fateful about those three words.

But then, that had been Peter.

Ben turned the page. There was a drawing of Ravenhill Court, an overhead view showing the nine homes, each home labeled with the name of the family living there. Surrounding the neighborhood, locations had been precisely labeled: Blue Clay Ravine, Ravenhill Ridge, Nike Base, Pirate's Cove, and others.

On the next page were hand-drawn images of young people, their names written beneath them. Ben laid a hand gently on the drawings: Peter, Julie, Louis, and Ben. He had been about thirteen at the time. He hadn't realized how good an artist Peter had been.

The next few pages held drawings of others from the neighborhood: Professor LaMothe, Mrs. Murray, Ben's mom and dad, Danny Bigalow, the Margolis brothers, Tony and Mike; Charlene. Each drawing was painstakingly labeled.

There were drawings then of some of the places where it had all taken place... images that brought the memories flooding back, memories of events that he hadn't so much forgotten, but that no longer seemed real. They were of a very different place and time. He saw the gnarled tree; a creek disappearing beneath overhanging brush; a cliff with a narrow ledge two-thirds of the way up; and there were the great, metal doors set into a hillside...

Ben Foster turned the page again...

Chapter One

June 1964

Ben Foster made the tight corner off Edgewood and into Ravenhill Court, the metal wheels of his red skateboard just touching the edge of the curb as he leaned heavily into it and swung back to the middle of the sidewalk. He rushed past the first house and turned down the driveway and onto the street. The sound of the wheels changed from a smooth roar to a low rumble as they rolled from concrete to asphalt. He lifted one foot off the board and shifted easily from rider to walker. Moving his schoolbook from one hand to the other, he reached down and picked up the skateboard. He continued across the street toward his house.

"Ben?" Mrs. Murray was standing at her front door. The Murray house was behind him, directly across the street from the Foster house. "Ben... where's Peter?"

"Hey, Mrs. Murray," Ben called out over his shoulder. "He had to stay after."

"Not again..."

Ben shrugged his shoulders and kept walking. He reached the short, steep driveway and started up, walked into the open garage of the Foster house. It was a roomy, two-car garage, with a 1960 Chevy Impala taking up the right half. A lawn mower was parked against one wall, with an assortment of lawn and garden tools hanging on the wall above it. Two Schwinn Sting-Ray bicycles were parked in front of a workbench; one a boy's bike, the other a girl's.

Ben set his skateboard down on the bench and continued on into the house, taking the two steps up and through the door to the kitchen. He dropped his book onto the table and went straight to the cupboard.

"I'm home," he called out dutifully. He took a glass down from the cupboard and filled it at the faucet.

His mother called back from somewhere at the back of the house. "How was your day?"

"Peter got in trouble again." Ben set the glass in the sink and walked out of the kitchen, started down the hall. Mrs. Foster came of Julie's room with a bundle of clothes in her arms.

"I don't know why your sister insists on living like a pig," she said.

"Hey, when you adopt, you never know what you're gonna get."

Mrs. Foster gave Ben a pointed look as they passed each other in the hall. "Julie is not adopted, and I wish you would quit saying that."

Ben reached the open back door. He pushed the screen door open and jumped past the step, landing on the back lawn. As the screen door slapped shut, he heard his mother cry out, "Get your schoolbook off my kitchen table!"

Ben was already approaching the back fence. He pushed the gate open and hurried through. It closed behind him with a banging clatter. He followed the well-traveled trail that ran along the back fences of the Ravenhill Court neighborhood. Tall, thick brush lined the right side of the trail.

He passed the Bigalow's back yard. The trail turned to the right. Before cutting back to follow along the Addison's fence, Ben left the trail and squeezed through the brush, trying as best he could to not leave any sign. Six steps in, he pushed some branches aside, revealing the weathered wood of a small door, about three and a half feet high and two feet wide. A shiny combination lock with a black dial hung on a latch. Ben reached in and began turning the knob on the lock.

Once inside the fort, he closed the door behind him and slid the inside latch to lock it.

The main room of the fort was a good eight feet wide by ten feet long. In the center of the room sat a wooden table and three chairs. A bench along one wall was made of two wooden boxes and a heavy plank. There were crude shelves on most of the walls with books and a number of odds and ends. Ben lit several thick candles that rested on their own short, narrow shelves.

A window, six inches high and eighteen inches wide, was set into the wall above the bench. Thick glass was set into the window opening and was held in place by an old picture frame. A wooden ladder was nailed to the wall in the far corner of the room, leading up to a small opening in the ceiling and a small square room on the second floor. The small room was large enough for a chair and little else.

Ben heard rustling outside, then the secret knock at the door. He reached over and pulled the latch aside. As Ben stepped back and sat on the bench, Peter came in and latched the door behind him.

"What are you doing here?"

Peter sat at the table with a loud grunt. "Hey, what can they do to me?"

Ben raised his gaze to look directly at Peter. They were both thirteen, but Peter was smaller and looked younger.

"You didn't go home?"

"No."

"Your mom was asking about you."

There was more rustling outside, and the secret knock. Instead of going to the door, Peter went to the ladder and climbed up into the tower. Ben went to the door and slid aside the latch, pulled the door open.

"Hey, Julie," he said.

"Hey." Julie went to the table. As she sat down, she peered up toward to the tower.

"Yeah," said Ben. He locked the door and returned to the bench. "He's here."

"Some real boss moves, Peter," Julie called out.

"Whatever," groaned Peter.

Ben smiled and leaned back, rested his head against the wall. "Don't be mean."

"Come on, Ben." Julie was a year older than Ben, but they could have passed for twins. "He stood up in class, during a test no less, and said *they're coming.*"

"It wasn't like that," said Ben. He had been there. After a few moments, "Okay... it was like that, but--"

Peter called down from the tower, "Don't make it sound so weird."

"It was weird," said Julie. "The whole school thinks you're peculiar."

Ben suddenly held a hand up for quiet. Julie turned her head to listen. There was only quiet. Ben shook his hand at her and listened more intently.

Up in the tower, Peter was looking through narrow slits set into the wall at eye level. The tower itself was hidden by the thick brush growing up around the fort. Peter wasn't able to see anyone yet, but he could hear a voice. It was coming from the direction of the trail. Then, as they came around the bend in the trail, Peter saw them. He clinched his teeth and held his breath.

It was Tony Margolis and his pet worm Danny Bigalow. Danny was in the same class as Peter and Ben.

"...and Miss Harris sent him to the principal," said Danny. He had a huge, rat grin on his face. "And Walker sent him to the nurse. And he was supposed to see the dean after school, but guess what? He didn't show up."

Tony Margolis was two years older than Danny. He listened quietly to the kid's unbounded glee.

"Man, oh man," said Danny. "It was so boss."

They reached the point in the trail where the hidden path forked off and led to the fort. They continued past along the main trail.

"What did he mean?" asked Tony, his eyes on the trail.

"Don't know. Maybe he told Walker." Danny bubbled with joy. "He is so weird."

Tony spoke as if to himself, "He is a strange little creep, all right."

They disappeared around the curve of the trail. Peter watched until he was sure they were gone, then climbed the ladder down into the main room.

Ben watched him, noting his expressionless face. He knew that look. He had known Peter all his life. Peter was working hard to keep it all down. He didn't want anyone to know that he was hurting.

"They're gone," said Peter. "Tony and his toady."

Ben nodded. "We heard."

Julie moved to another chair so Peter could sit down. "How can he let that weasel pant after him like that?"

"We are witness to hero worship at its most disgusting," said Peter. "Tony Margolis eats it up. It's what he lives for."

"Tony's nothing like his brother," said Ben.

"Mike's all right, I guess," said Peter. "Hard to believe they're related."

"Tony was adopted," said Ben.

"Ben!" Julie said sharply. She was getting really, really tired of this adoption stuff.

Peter grinned, leaned over the table. "You know, Julie, you and Tony do bear a striking resemblance. Perhaps--"

"Funny. Did that come to you in another of your visions?"

The three of them grew suddenly very quiet. Ben gave Julie a stern look. In the silence, he could hear the sounds of the candle wicks sizzling in their pools of liquid wax. The tiny flames flickered and sent shadows dancing across their faces. Ben let out a breath he hadn't known he was holding.

"Tell us what you saw, Peter."

Peter looked at Ben, then Julie. He wanted to tell them. He always told them. There was something about this one, though. It was different; different, and yet not different. They were always different, sort of. This one... this one was... *bad.*

"It was like a doorway," he said. "It was a... gateway..."

"What kind of gateway?" Julie slid nearer. "To where?"

"Like a door. Like an open door. It glowed. Blue. I saw shadows on the other side. Shadows of..." Peter tried to see what lay just beyond, but he couldn't seem to reach it.

"What... like monsters?" asked Ben.

Peter shook his head, discouraged.

"Go on," said Julie. "What were the shadows doing?"

"I think they were trying to come through, but something was stopping them."

"Do you know why they wanted to come through?"

"No," said Peter. He looked directly at Julie then, and spoke certainly. "No. But it didn't feel right."

Ben let out another heavy breath. "His visions may not always be right, but the feelings that he gets about 'em usually are."

Julie looked back at Peter, "What made you, ya' know... jump up like that... in class?"

"Yeah," said Ben. "We try to keep your weirdness just between us. Ya' know?"

"No sense in letting the whole world know how peculiar you are," said Julie.

Peter shifted about nervously. This was the different part. This was what made this vision so very different from the others.

"This time... this one... this one was... *different.*"

"Different how?"

"One of the shadows reached out..." He looked quickly from Ben to Julie, then back to Ben. They squirmed impatiently.

"Yeah?" Ben urged.

"You know... from the other side. It reached out... It touched me; on the shoulder."

Chapter Two

The next morning was like most Saturday mornings in the Foster house. When Ben came into the kitchen, he found his dad at the breakfast table reading a newspaper, a cup of coffee sitting on the table in front of him, dressed as if planning the spend the day kickin' around the house. His mom was standing at the counter buttering slices of toast.

"Good morning, Ben." She placed the dish of toast onto the table.

"'morning." He watched as she returned to the counter, poured a glass of orange juice and set it in front of him. He continued to watch as she went to the cupboard and brought back the box of Cheerios, then a cereal bowl, a spoon, and finally the milk from the refrigerator.

"Eat your breakfast," she said absently.

"Thanks, Mom."

"Good morning," said Julie, coming into the kitchen.

Ben continued to watch silently as Saturday morning methodically played itself out.

"Good morning, Julie," said Mom. She poured a glass of juice and set it in front of Julie.

"Good morning, sweetie," said Dad from behind his newspaper.

Mom took a cereal bowl down from the cupboard, a spoon from the drawer, and set them in front of Julie. "Eat your breakfast."

"Thanks, Mom."

Ben and Julie filled their bowls with Cheerios and milk and began eating. Mrs. Foster fussed about cleaning up the counter before sitting down herself to coffee and toast. Mr. Foster continued reading the newspaper, occasionally reaching around for his coffee cup or another slice of toast.

"So," said Mrs. Foster, watching her children spoon cereal into their mouths and Mr. Foster as he absently searched for his coffee cup. "How does everyone plan to spend their day?"

Ben shrugged. "Hang out."

"Me, too," said Julie.

"Mmm," said Dad.

Mom gave the newspaper a sharp look. "Honey?"

"How's Peter?" he asked, without lowering the paper.

"Okay," said Ben.

"Weird," said Julie.

Mom shook her head sadly, sipped her coffee.

"He's not weird," said Ben. He leaned forward and grabbed a slice of toast from the stack. "Okay, so he's weird."

"That poor boy," said Mom, smiling sympathetically. She gave the newspaper another sharp look. "He hasn't had a father to help him, the way you two have."

Mr. Foster ignored the subtle jab, and apparently also the conversation that was going on beyond the newspaper. "They're dropping off the Mercury this morning."

"Hmm," said Mrs. Foster, not particularly pleased.

"You kids make sure the garage is clear," said Dad.

"No problem," said Ben.

"The game is on the radio this afternoon," said Mr. Foster.

"I don't know why you bought that old thing," said Mrs. Foster.

Mr. Foster gave a pleasant sigh, lowered the paper and gave his wife a gentle look. "What better way to spend an afternoon? Tinkering under the hood of a grand old automobile... listening to the ballgame..."

"What happened to Peter's father?" Julie asked suddenly. Mom and Dad gave each other a quick glance and there was an uncomfortable, if brief, moment of silence.

Ben's mouth was full of Cheerios. "He just up and disappeared," he mumbled.

"No one knows what happened, dear," said Mom.

"Peter never talks about it," said Julie. "All we know is that he disappeared."

Ben watched curiously as Mom gave Dad another very quick glance before picking up her coffee cup and taking another sip. She held the cup in front of her face as she spoke. "Peter was just a baby at the time," she said. "John left for work one morning and never came home."

"Did ya know him?"

"Very well."

"What was he like?"

"Peculiar?" asked Ben, smiling. "Like Peter?"

"John Murray was a good man," said Dad. He gave the newspaper a stern shake and turned the page, was once again hidden from view. "A good man."

"He was a very gentle man," said Mom.

Julie looked thoughtfully at her half-empty bowl of Cheerios, stirred the floating cereal with her spoon. "Some of the kids are thinking, you know, with Peter being... like he is... that maybe his father just..."

"Not at all," said Mom.

"Claptrap," said Dad from behind the newspaper. "Nonsense."

Ben watched the shifting newspaper for some further comment, but none came. He looked then at Mom, who was just looking away from Dad. She gave Ben a slight smile and carefully set the cup down in front of her. Ben smiled back, then stood and took his cereal bowl and juice glass to the sink.

"Gotta go," he said.

Mrs. Murray had finished her breakfast of eggs and toast, was staring absently across the table at Peter. She cradled her lukewarm coffee in one hand and held a cigarette in the other. Peter ignored her, busily wiped the egg yolk from his plate with a half-slice of toast.

There was a heavy knock at the kitchen door. Mrs. Murray gave the door only a casual glance before Peter called out. "Come in."

"Hey, Peter," said Ben. He left the door open, but let the screen door slap shut behind him. "Good Morning, Mrs. Murray."

"Hey," said Peter.

"Good morning, Ben," said Mrs. Murray. She was wearing a long white robe and fluffy slippers, had her hair brushed back and pulled into a pony tail.

Ben plopped himself down in the nearest chair. The tiny kitchen smelled of fried eggs, toast and butter, cigarette smoke, and the ever-present half-filled ashtray sitting within easy reach beside Mrs. Murray's breakfast plate.

Peter stood up quickly and stuffed the last of his toast into his mouth. "I'm done," he said. He carried his plate to the sink while washing the toast down with the last of his juice.

Mrs. Murray gave Peter a motherly look. "Don't rush, sweetie. You'll make yourself sick."

"Gotta go, Mom." Peter was at the screen door and out.

Ben hurried after him, calling back, "Bye, Mrs. Murray."

Mrs. Murray stared at the closing door. The kitchen was quiet again; a slight breeze coming in from outside pushed the cigarette smoke away from her face. She tapped the ash into the ashtray and took another sip of her coffee.

Ben caught up with Peter out on the sidewalk. The morning was clear and sunny. Across the street, the garage door to the Foster house was open and Ben could see his dad moving about inside. Over at the Margolis house, Mike Margolis was climbing into his 58 Chevy. Further down the street, Mr. Addison was bringing out his lawnmower. At the Bigalow house, Mr. Bigalow was standing out on his lawn, wrapped in an old robe, giving his newspaper the once-over.

Saturday was getting started in Ravenhill Court.

Julie came out of the Foster house through the garage, walked down the driveway and crossed the street.

"Hey," she said.

"Hey," said Peter.

Julie looked up the street. Mike had started his car and was letting it warm up. Mr. Addison was trying to get his lawnmower started. Mr. Bigalow was scratching at his backside as he headed in the general direction of his front door.

"You guys ready?" she asked.

" 'course not," said Peter.

Ben frowned. "If anyone knows what's going on, it'll be the Professor."

"I suppose," said Peter.

"Yeah," said Julie.

"The Professor is a good guy."

"I never said different."

They all turned at the sound of a door closing. Donna Osborne had come out of her house next door and was staring at the three of them from her porch. She gave Peter a big, jeering grin. "Hey, Peter, seen any Martians?"

"Just the big one I'm lookin' at."

"Shut up, Donna," said Ben.

Donna continued eyeing Peter. "Are these your Martian comrades?"

"You're such an ignoramus," said Julie.

"Why do you hang out with these losers, Julie? Ya' can't get any real friends?"

Mike Margolis had backed his car out of his driveway. He drove it past the group on his way out of Ravenhill Court. Donna smiled broadly and waved as he passed. Mike ignored all of them.

"Let's go," said Ben. He started up the street toward Professor LaMothe's house. Peter and Julie followed after him.

Once Donna was certain that Mike had gone, she turned her attention back to Peter and his moron friends.

"Hey, Peter! You let me know if you see any aliens, eh?"

Up in the heart of the Court, Mr. Addison had begun mowing his yard. Mr. Bigalow had gone back into his house. At Mrs. Weatherby's house, a twirling sprinkler spun slowly, watering a small circle of lawn.

Everything was normal.

Everything was 1964, small-town America.

Chapter Three

Mrs. LaMothe was small in stature, and a rather demure woman, but she carried herself with a sophisticated presence that insisted her station in society was above whatever her surroundings might imply. She had done what she could with the simple, middle-class home that she found herself living in, and there was a definite contrast between the neighborhood outside and the home inside. There was a calm elegance within, with lace and crystal, fine woods and thick, tasteful carpet.

She walked across the front room as if someone might be watching and opened the door. She looked down, as best her height would allow, at the three young people standing on her large, covered porch.

"Hello, Mrs. LaMothe," said Ben.

"Good morning, Benjamin," said Mrs. LaMothe warily. She gave each of the children a studied look. "How can I help you?"

"We would like to see the Professor, please," said Julie.

"A bit early for callers, young lady."

"It's kind of important, ma'am," said Peter.

Mrs. LaMothe gave Peter another studied look and a raised brow. She turned her gaze again to Ben, knowing that whatever they were about, Benjamin Foster was the likely instigator.

"Professor LaMothe is in his den," she said. She made no effort to move aside, leaving them to stand uncertainly on the porch, waiting for some sign to enter. She finally turned about in one sweeping motion and started away from the door. "This way. Close the door behind you."

She led them from the front hall and across the main living area. All was prim and proper, and far too refined to be touched. They held their arms close at their sides. A clock on a shelf loudly ticked off the passing seconds.

She opened the door to the professor's den. The room was as different from the rest of the house as the house was from the neighborhood. It was a world unto itself, large and filled with deep shadows and the smells of old paper and book leather. Scattered haphazardly about the room were old lamps of various designs, assorted side tables and high-back wooden chairs, and the professor's large roll-top desk with its cubbyholes crammed with papers and odds-and-ends. The walls were floor-to-ceiling shelves filled with books, and on the tables were dozens of old leather-bound volumes, brought down from the shelves in times past and never returned.

Mrs. LaMothe spoke officiously, "Professor LaMothe, you have guests."

The professor looked up from a large, dusty book and twisted about in his chair. There was a loud squeaking sound as he leaned forward. He answered with a bit of mocking officiousness.

"Thank you... Mrs. LaMothe."

Mrs. LaMothe raised a brow, backed out of the room and closed the door. The professor smiled.

"Welcome, welcome." He gave Peter a sparkling sharp eye. "I hear you've been spreading fear and unrest, young Master Murray."

"No, sir."

"Hmm." The professor leaned back. His chair let out more painful squeals. He waved his hands about for the three to come nearer and find places to sit. He watched each of them closely as they struggled to clear chairs of piles of books. Once they were settled in, he looked directly at Ben. Ben looked first at the others, then spoke forcefully.

"He sees things, Professor."

"So I understand."

"And he can sense things. He feels things."

The professor's stare made Ben uncomfortable, but he didn't turn away. He had known Professor LaMothe all his life, and he had been in this room many times. He liked the professor. And he knew that the professor liked him. The professor was a brilliant man, and he knew things that no normal person knew.

Ben also understood that when the professor looked at you, he was seeing things that no normal person saw. It was just the way he was. All Ben could do was look right back.

Professor LaMothe turned his gaze on Peter. "And what did you see yesterday, Peter?"

"I..." Peter looked to Ben for support. Ben only nodded encouragingly. Peter turned back to the professor. "I saw a doorway."

Professor LaMothe shifted imperceptibly, and the chair let out a short squeak. "No ordinary doorway, I wager."

"No, sir."

"A gateway, perhaps."

The children all perked up. Julie eyed the professor suspiciously, but said nothing. Professor LaMothe gave her a quick glance and slight nod, but kept his attention on Peter.

"A portal to... someplace else," he said, his tone flat.

"Yessir."

"How could you know that, Professor?" asked Julie.

The professor leaned back heavily, taking in the chair's answering cry. He continued to watch Peter.

"We hoped you could tell us what it means," said Ben.

Professor LaMothe looked as if he was sorting through a library of thoughts, finally gave Ben a reassuring smile. "I will tell you what I can, of course."

"Then you do know what's going on."

"I should be able to give you a good start on finding the answers that you are seeking."

"What does that mean?" asked Julie. There was something really, *really* fishy about this.

Professor LaMothe let his gaze wander over the book-lined walls of his den. He would have to handle this very carefully.

How much to tell the children?

"It has been a very long time... but the reappearance of the gateway is not unexpected."

"It's been here before?" asked Ben.

"Oh, yes. It has most definitely been here before."

"Is it bad?"

"In and of themselves, the gateways are not bad. They do, however, portend *interesting* times ahead."

"And what does that mean?" Julie's question was more of a frustrating demand. "You're not telling us anything, Professor."

Ben shot Julie an angry look, but the professor only smiled kindly. Peter sat silent and unmoving, not taking his eyes off the professor. The professor gave Peter another reassuring nod and turned to Julie.

"I am sorry. I suppose I do sound a bit cryptic."

"She's just like that, Professor," said Ben.

"No, no," said the professor. "Your sister is quite right, and I do apologize. I said I would tell you what I can, and I certainly will."

What I can, Julie thought. *He said 'what I can'. What does he know that he can't tell us?*

"There just seems to be a lot of strange stuff going on these days, Professor," said Ben. "And Peter usually sees it coming."

"Did you see anything inside the gateway, son?" The professor asked Peter.

"Just shadows."

"Did you sense anything from these shadows?"

"One reached out," said Ben. "It touched him."

"Yes?" asked the professor, not really surprised.

Peter only nodded.

"Please, Professor," said Julie.

For several long moments, he kept his gaze on Peter, probing, seeking, looking for something. Then, as if he had found what he wanted, he leaned back and calmly turned so that he was looking in the general direction of the window across the room, though he was looking at nothing in particular.

"Ravenhill Court is a very special place, Miss Foster. I have no doubt that you already know that. We who live here are a part of what makes this place special. Young Peter, of all of us, is most special indeed."

"How, why, what? I'm sorry, Professor, but you're still not telling us anything."

"I tell you what I can."

"But not necessarily what you know."

"Julie!" Ben hissed.

"Quite all right, Ben," said the professor. "Your sister is very perceptive."

"Sir?"

The professor spoke directly to Julie. "I don't have all the answers, Julie. I in fact have many questions of my own. I am hoping that you can help me answer some of them. And, perhaps, with these answers, will come those that you yourself are seeking."

Peter cleared his throat, as if trying to catch someone's attention. "What do you want us to do, Professor?"

"I need for you find that gateway, son."

"It isn't open," said Peter. "Not now. I can't see it."

"It will open again."

"How do we find it?" asked Ben. He hadn't thought that it actually existed, not as a real thing that you could walk up to and touch.

"Peter will find it for you. It won't be far away." The professor began rummaging through the drawers and cubby holes of his desk.

"Why won't you tell us more?" Julie pleaded.

"What do we do when we find it?" asked Ben. "Are we supposed to go through it?"

"No." Professor LaMothe said quickly, then returned to his hunt. "Do not go through the gateway."

"Professor LaMothe!" Julie demanded.

The professor found what he was looking for. It was a small, black cloth bag with a tie string. He turned back to the children and held it out in the palm of one hand.

"You must take this to the gateway."

"Why?" Julie asked sharply. "What is it?"

The professor tossed the bag to Julie. She opened it and pulled out a crystal the size of a large walnut. She studied it carefully, and held it out for the others to see.

"That crystal must get to the other side of the gateway," said the professor.

"But you can't tell us why."

"I'm sorry, Miss Foster. Please be patient. The answers will come."

Ben had the crystal now. "We'll do it, Professor." He handed it back to Julie, who dropped it back into the bag.

Professor LaMothe set a hand palm down onto the top of his desk and looked across at Peter. "Now... Julie, hand Peter the crystal."

"Oh-kay..." Julie handed the bag over to Peter with a mocking delicacy.

"Peter, this is important. You must be the one to get the crystal to the other side... but you must wait until you know the time is right."

"I don't know..."

"You will. Do not give up the crystal until you know the time is right."

Peter stared anxiously at the professor, but Ben spoke up firmly.

"We'll take care of it, Professor," he said.

"I know you will." The professor's gaze glided slowly across the three of them. "One more thing,"

"Here it comes," said Julie.

"You will in all probability not be the only ones searching for the gateway."

"What?"

"Their goal and yours are not the same. At least, not exactly. You must get there first, and you must get the crystal through."

"Are these guys dangerous?"

The professor seemed to struggle for an answer. "They have no desire to harm you, but they are sincere in their efforts and will do whatever is necessary to stop you from getting the crystal across."

"Why?" asked Julie.

Again the professor struggled for an adequate answer. "Opinions differ as to how to resolve our problem."

"What problem?" Julie was growing more frustrated by the moment.

The professor's response was very long in coming.

"I'm sorry."

Chapter Four

Ben was the second one to the fort the next morning. Peter was already there and had to open the door for him. Once inside, he set the scout backpack on the table and Peter began loading it up with the supplies that he had gathered.

"Be careful. There's sandwiches in there," said Ben. "I don't want 'em all squished."

"Anything to drink?"

"We'll take a canteen."

"That'll work," said Peter. "We can fill it up at the creek."

"Is that where we're going?"

Peter stopped packing. "I think so," he said.

They heard the secret knock at the door, and Ben pulled back the latch to let Julie in.

"Hey," she said, latching the door behind her.

"Hey," said Peter.

"Man, it's really foggy out there."

"Did Mom say anything?" asked Ben.

"Nah. I think her and Dad had a fight about the new car."

Peter grinned. "That is one really butt-ugly piece of automobile."

"It's a classic," Julie said, mocking her father.

"I think it's kinda' boss," said Ben.

"Maybe Dad will leave it to you in his will."

Peter closed up the day pack, stared at it and took two deep breaths. "That's it. I'm as ready as I'll ever be."

"So let's split," said Julie.

Once back on the trail, they followed it past the Addison's backyard and on around to the Weatherby's, where the trail forked. Following the left fork would have taken them around behind the houses on the other side of Ravenhill Court. They took the right fork instead, which took them inland along Raven's Creek. In most places, the creek was narrow enough that a hop-skip-and-jump could take them from one side to the other with barely a splash. Low rolling hills rose up on either side.

The morning was gray and the air was damp. Mossy branches hung heavy over the stream and the winding trail that followed it, blocking out what little light there was and keeping Ben, Julie and Peter in shadows most of the time. For the first few hundred yards, the only sound was that of snapping twigs as they pushed aside the brush and low-hanging branches, and the occasional splash as they were forced off the trail and into the water. They wanted to put some distance between themselves and the neighborhood before they spoke. It was still pretty early on a quiet Sunday morning, and they were afraid that their voices would carry all the way out onto the street. They didn't want to draw attention to themselves.

Ben was leading the way, with Julie not far behind and Peter following clumsily along after them. He had first shift with the backpack.

"There's the clearing," said Ben. The brush was as thick as ever and closed in tight to the creek, but there was a bright opening up ahead. It was the first major clearing on Raven's Creek and a common location for those traveling the trail to stop and dry out, readjust their gear and get set for the next leg. For many, it was the final destination, being an out-of-the-way hangout not too far from the neighborhood.

For the last few yards before the clearing, the trail ran directly alongside the creek and was wet and slippery. Ben had to dance some careful maneuvers to not fall in and hopped the last steps out into the brightening gray morning. He stopped suddenly, and Julie and then Peter both jumped off-balance to one side in order not to run into him.

Ben was staring at Louis Bennett, who sat quietly on a small hillock at the far edge of the clearing.

"Hey," said Louis. He was in the eighth grade with Ben and Peter, but was a year younger. He lived on the corner next door to Ben. The Bennetts were the only black family in the neighborhood. In fact, they were the only black family that Ben knew personally.

"Hey," he said back. Over the surprise, he walked into the center of the clearing and called back to Peter, "How about that canteen? The water's clearest over there." He pointed to a wide spot in the creek where the water ran over some river-rock.

"Yeah, yeah... gimme a sec," said Peter. He was struggling to get the day pack off. Julie finally went over to help. Meanwhile, Ben was looking at Louis and Louis was looking up at Ben.

"Whatcha' doin' here, Louis?"

"Hangin'."

"Yeah?" Ben was doubtful.

"Yeah." The gray skies were continuing to brighten and Louis had to squint now to keep eye-to-eye with Ben. The fog was going to burn off early.

"How long ya' plan on *hangin'*?"

Louis shrugged. "Bit longer." He smiled.

Ben smiled back. "Give, Louis..."

Louis' smile broadened. He finally looked away and shrugged. "Prof thought I should come along."

"Along?"

"With you guys." Louis looked up at Julie's approach. She stood beside her brother. Peter was kneeling at the creek, filling the canteen.

"What do you know of it?" asked Julie.

"A bit."

"What did LaMothe tell you?"

"Just that you guys were doing something important; that you might need me."

"Need you for what?" asked Ben.

Louis shrugged, leaned forward and stood up. He was four inches shorter than Ben. He brushed his pants clean and took a step closer to Ben. "Listen, man, I'm just doing what the Prof asked me. You think I like coming out here on a cold, wet morning and spending my Sunday traipsing around the hills with you guys?"

"Then why do it?" asked Julie. Unlike Ben and Louis, she had yet to smile.

"Because the Prof asked me to."

"You always do what the professor asks?"

"Yeah," said Louis. "I do."

"Why?"

Louis gave her a cool steady look. "Cause he's the Prof," he said. He watched Peter come up to them, struggling to get the cap back on the canteen.

He turned his attention back to Julie. "I see that <u>you're</u> out here, on this wet, gray morning... just as the professor told you."

"Ouch," said Ben.

"I'm out here because Peter needs us," said Julie. "Whatever Professor LaMothe is after, I'm here to watch Peter's back."

The four of them stood silent. Peter began to look uncomfortable. Louis finally gave a short, curt nod.

"I dig that," he said quietly.

"Cool," said Ben, flatly. He turned then and started across the clearing. "Let's go."

His sudden departure took the others by surprise and they had to scramble to follow after him. Peter picked up the backpack and trailed after the others, holding the pack out in front of him.

"Hey! Hey, you guys! Somebody else's turn with this. Hey!"

The trail stayed close to the meandering creek, veering off only when it had to, when the brush grew too thick or large boulders pushed up from the ground, or the banks rose up too steeply. They followed the trail for several hours, spoke only occasionally, sometimes mumbling a warning of nearby poison oak or some other danger, but more often a comment on near-miss stumbles with near-miraculous recoveries that saved one and then another of them from making the big splash.

At each clearing along the way they would stop and look to Peter. At each clearing Peter would say only *'Not far... up ahead.'* The small pack would change hands and they would go on. Ben continued to lead the way.

They stopped for lunch at a large clearing with several fallen logs and a number of circles of rocks where people had made campfires. It was only eleven o'clock, but this was as far as any of them had ever traveled Raven's Creek, and they didn't know if there would be another good spot further on to take a break. At the far end of the clearing, the stream disappeared once again into thick brush and low-hanging trees and shadows.

Julie sat with Peter on one log, some distance from Ben and Louis. This gave Ben an opportunity to share a sandwich and ask Louis more about how and why Professor LaMothe had asked him to join them.

Louis had shown up at the LaMothe house the previous afternoon to mow their yard. In addition to his own yard, Ben knew that Louis had the LaMothe house and Mrs. Weatherby's, as well as several others over on Edgewood.

He had finished the front lawn and was pushing the mower around to the back yard when the professor called him into his den. Ben could just imagine what Mrs. LaMothe thought of a neighborhood kid tracking freshly cut grass into the house, but Louis didn't say anything about it.

The professor had told Louis that Ben, Julie and Peter were going to be traveling up Raven's Creek the next morning, and that what they were doing was very important. He asked Louis if he would be available to go with them, to help them if he could. The professor told Louis that his help might be needed on this journey or the next. He warned that it might be dangerous, but that the future of Ravenhill Court was at stake.

Louis didn't know what Prof meant by *'this journey or the next'*, and when Ben asked how the professor knew that they would be traveling up Raven's Creek, Louis said that he thought that's where Prof had told them to go.

Hadn't he told them where to go?

Ben knew they hadn't talked about where the gateway was. He remembered specifically that the professor had told them that Peter would know how to find it.

Then he remembered... the professor hadn't actually said that he didn't know where the gateway was, only that Peter would be able to find it.

Then it was Ben's turn to fill Louis in on what little he knew. Louis had pretty much figured out that it had to have been something to do with the scene that Peter had made at school, but the gateway thing and the deal with the crystal was news to him. The professor hadn't told him anything about it. And while he had said that it might get dangerous, he hadn't told Louis that there might be others out here trying to stop what the professor had sent them out to do.

Once he had laid out the whole story to Louis, Ben asked if he still wanted come along. He felt Louis deserved the chance to back out. Ben didn't believe that he should have to face what they might be facing without at least having the few facts that he could give him, however few they might be.

Ben found that he was strangely relieved when Louis said that he would continue on with them. If anything, Louis was more determined than ever to go on. Ben realized then that, despite the fact that the kid was a year younger and smaller, with Louis along he was just a little less anxious about what might lay ahead.

For as long as he could remember, it had always been Ben and Julie and Peter. Having an outsider in their midst had at first been unsettling. They had all felt it. They liked Louis well enough, but no one could simply walk in and suddenly be one of them. Still, by the time they had stopped for lunch, and certainly by the time they had finished lunch, Ben was at least okay with having Louis around, whether he was one of them or not.

They started out again, Ben continuing to lead, with Peter guiding them ever forward. From here on out, the trail was used mostly by deer and smaller animals, only occasionally by people. Being less traveled, it was less well-defined, but still easy enough to follow. There were also fewer trees, but the brush was thicker and taller. There were fewer clearings, but the sky was more visible, with the openings overhead coming more frequently.

Twenty minutes from the lunch clearing, the trail turned down toward the brook and stopped at the water's edge. Ben saw several stones in the water and the trail continuing on the other side. He looked back at the others, then at Peter.

Peter confidently pointed upstream. Ben saw something in Peter's expression. There was something different. Something had changed. Peter was sensing something...

Ben leapt from the bank, hopped from one stone to the other and reached the other side, the others following quickly behind. Several yards on, the trail turned away from the bank, winding away until the brook was no longer visible. The brush on either side of the trail was twice as tall as Ben, and the last of the trees were left behind. The fog was gone and the sky overhead was light blue.

Ben stopped suddenly, frozen in midstride. The others stopped where they were, either because they had heard what he had heard or they could see that he had heard something.

Someone or something was out there.

It was too quiet to be in the brush. It was either up ahead on the same trail they were traveling, or maybe on another one nearby.

Ben indicated to the others that they should wait where they were. He moved off then, quickly and quietly down the trail. He rounded a bend and stopped at the next. He knelt behind a bush and carefully peeked around the corner.

A man was stepping down onto the trail from another steep path that wound down from the hillside. He was dressed in rugged outdoor garb and a military cap. Following after him were three men in military khakis. All wore sidearms.

Once on the trail, they headed away from Ben, quickly disappearing around the next bend.

"Who are they?" whispered Julie, close enough that Ben felt her breath on his ear. Ben almost jumped into the bushes.

"I told you to stay where you were."

"Yeah? Who died and made you boss?"

The others scrambled up behind Julie.

"What are they doing here?" asked Louis.

Ben looked irritated. "I imagine the same thing we are; looking for the gateway."

"I'll bet they're the ones the professor was talking about," said Peter.

"Ya' think?"

"LaMothe needs to spill it about what's going on," said Julie. She jabbed a finger in the direction the men had taken. "That was a government spook."

"A spy?" asked Louis. "Really?"

"Some kind of a special agent... and with a military escort, no less."

Peter stood up slowly. He looked half-dazed. The others stood then, knowing that something was up, half expecting him to go into another of his weird fits.

"Peter?" Ben finally asked.

"It's open," he said.

Ben looked up the trail, in the direction the government man and his escort had gone. He turned back to Peter. "Do you know where it is? Can you get us there?"

Peter nodded.

"Okay," said Ben. "We gotta get there first."

Chapter Five

They hoped to find a spot where they could get around the four men, and then once past them to hurry down the trail as fast as they could. The problem was, the trail offered not only the easiest travel, but also the most direct route down the valley. Getting around the men, who were traveling that trail, wasn't going to be easy.

They followed along at a safe distance, waiting for their chance. They had gone about a quarter of a mile when Peter tapped Ben on the shoulder. The trail twisted right, but Peter pointed straight ahead.

"Ya' sure?" Ben whispered.

Peter nodded and pointed. Straight ahead.

The brush wasn't too thick here, and it looked like the going wouldn't be too bad. The trail the government men were taking continued to follow along the creek bank.

"All right," said Ben, and led the way into the bushes.

Another few hundred yards and they came out of the brush near the opening to a narrow ravine that cut into the left slope of the valley. Ben gave Peter only a quick glance before going in.

The ravine was no more than eight or ten feet wide most of the way, occasionally widening out to form high-walled clearings filled with brush and large granite stones. The sun's rays reached down to the floor in narrow beams.

The floor of the ravine rose steadily as they continued forward, becoming steep in some places.

They heard voices behind them. The government man and his escort had found the ravine.

"Come on," said Ben and they picked up the pace. Behind them, the voices grew louder, grew nearer. They were gaining. It became clear to Ben that while they might get there first, there was no way they would be able to do anything before those coming up the ravine joined them.

There was a crevice in the wall up ahead. Ben ran to it and waved the others in, then hurriedly followed in after. He had just backed into the shadows of the fissure when the government man rounded the bend and approached, the three escort right behind him. They passed by the crevice without looking in and were gone.

Ben stepped out, and then the others.

"This isn't good," said Peter.

"Now what?" Julie whispered.

In answer, Ben started silently forward, hurrying after the four men but careful to stay out of sight.

They came up to a low wall that jutted out from one side of the ravine, crouched low and used it as cover.

The clearing beyond glowed a bright, clear blue. In the center stood the gateway, from which the glow emanated. It had the dimensions of a regular doorway, but looked completely transparent; Ben could see through the gateway to the rock walls of the clearing beyond.

The government man stood directly in front of the gateway, forming a dark silhouette before it, and the three military men stood at the edges of clearing, surrounding the shimmering object before them.

Peter looked entranced by the scene. After several moments huddled behind the wall, he stood and started around the others toward the heart of the clearing. Ben grabbed at him, just managing to hold onto him.

The government man sensed movement behind him and turned around. His face shimmered in the blue glow. He looked carefully at Peter. His appearance was calm and deliberate.

At the man's movement, the military men had turned to Peter as well, taking a defensive posture. At the slightest gesture of their leader, the men stopped and held their position.

The government man turned his attention back to the gateway. There were shadows moving about within it, movement as of someone walking across a room beyond the doorway. Everyone in the clearing stood very still. Over a period of several seconds, the shadows slowly took form, becoming finally the silhouette of a man. The government man looked calmly on, waiting patiently, the shimmering of light and shadow bringing the clearing to life.

◊ ◊ ◊

The man beyond the gateway stepped through, but kept his back just within the flickering light. He had the same internal glow of the gateway, but to all appearances looked to be completely normal. Peter took a step closer, with Ben and the others right behind him.

"Hello, Ashton," said the man from the gateway.

"Hello, John," said the government man.

John looked around the clearing. He saw the military escort that Ashton had brought with him, and then the young people standing five yards behind Ashton.

"Interesting welcoming committee." he said.

"I'm here to help, John."

John laughed sharply. He shook his head and studied Ashton. "All I need is the crystal," he said.

"I don't have it."

Peter started to speak up, but Ben stopped him. He remembered what the professor had said. *Wait until the time is right.*

"Then they will be lost," said John.

"Giving you the crystal won't help that," said the government man.

"It's the only thing that will."

"And if it fails?"

John looked frustrated, as if he had been fighting this same fight, arguing this same argument, for a very long time. "You must get me the crystal."

"Sorry, John. It isn't going to happen."

"Ashton, I can save them."

"John Murray, savior?"

Peter stiffened at hearing the name.

John Murray...

"Your father!" Julie hissed in a harsh whisper. Peter said nothing, but took another step closer.

John Murray shook his head sadly. "You know better than that, Ashton."

"I certainly do," said Ashton. The tone was accusatory. "You've done enough. We'll take it from here. Hopefully, we can salvage something from this mess."

Ben calmly placed the small black bag into Peter's hand. Peter gripped it tightly, took two guarded steps forward. He was within arm's reach of Ashton, standing off to one side. Ashton turned his head enough to watch the boy while still keeping an eye on John Murray. When one of the military escort started forward, Ashton held up a halting hand.

"You're my dad?" Peter asked the gateway man.

John Murray looked uncertainly at the boy. When he turned back to Ashton, the government man nodded. Murray let out a long breath.

"How long?" he asked.

"Almost twelve years on this side."

"We knew that there would be... but it can't..."

"Think about what that does to the calculations," said Ashton. "Think about what it means for <u>us</u>, John."

John Murray looked to Ashton for some further clarification, but nothing came. He looked over at Peter, took a step from the gateway. Still shrouded in the aura of the gateway, he knelt on one knee. Peter approached, looking down into the face of the father that he had never known. John Murray held out a hand.

"I'm sorry, son."

Peter placed his hand in his father's. The blue glow surrounding John Murray radiated out to Peter's hand and part way up his arm. John Murray's eyes sparkled imperceptibly as he felt the bag containing the crystal in Peter's hand.

Still looking at Peter, he spoke to the government man.

"I'll not let the boy down, Ashton," he said. He stood then and let go of Peter's hand. He took a step back. The gateway shimmered and flickered at John Murray's presence.

"We can work together, John."

"Apparently not," he said. He looked at Peter. "Tell the professor I said hello."

Peter could only nod, numbed by the strange turn of events.

Ashton pleaded, "John, please."

John Murray gave Ashton only a cursory glance, looked again at his son. "Six, three, six," he said, and took the final step back into the gateway. His image shifted to silhouette, then slowly dissolved to a mix of swimming shadows. The gateway darkened, and the eerie glow in the clearing began to fade. The gateway vanished. The clearing grew gray, almost colorless, with only a thin band of light from the weak afternoon sun reaching down to the floor of the ravine.

The three military men still stood around the edge of the clearing, surrounding Ashton and Peter. The others remained at a safe distance.

For several long seconds, no one moved, no one spoke. Ashton finally looked down at Peter, turned slowly about and gave Ben a long, studied look. Ben managed to hide a sudden dread. He had no idea what Ashton might do now.

"Wow," said Ben. "Bummer."

Ashton's expression was almost sad. "Yeah," he said finally. The sadness in his face was reflected in the tone of his voice.

"Well," Ben tried to smile. "I guess we gotta split."

He took a step back, watching for some reaction from Ashton. Julie and Louis stepped back with him. Ben stiffly waved for Peter to follow. Peter had trouble moving his legs, but finally got the first foot out, then the other. Using only his eyes, Ashton let his men know to hold their positions and let the kids go. Once they were gone, Ashton turned back to where the gateway had been.

"Bummer," he mumbled to himself.

Chapter Six

Ben was sitting on the bench in the fort, his back against the wall. Peter sat at the table scribbling in his new journal. He had picked it up at the variety store right after school the day before and had hardly taken his nose out of it since.

He spoke up while still writing. "Maybe it's a combination," he said.

"Combination, maybe, but not to any ordinary lock," said Ben.

"I think the professor knows, no matter what he said."

Julie called out then from her place up in the tower. "Here comes Louis."

Ben slid down the bench toward the door. When he heard the secret knock, he opened it and let Louis in, latched it shut behind him.

"Hey, guys," said Louis. He looked admiringly around the room. "Cool."

"Welcome," said Peter, only briefly looking up from his journal.

Ben slid back to his place on the bench. "Well?"

Louis sat down beside him and shook his head. "No sign of Prof anywhere."

"Where's he gone off to?" Ben asked sullenly.

"Ya' think he's hiding?"

Julie climbed down from the tower. "*Hiding* is definitely the operative word," she said.

"Wherever he's hiding," said Ben, "or *whatever* he's hiding, he's still on our side. We don't want to lose sight of that."

"What's the good of having him on our side if he doesn't tell us anything?" Julie sat down opposite Peter and glanced curiously at the pictures he was drawing in the journal. One of them looked a lot like her.

Ben was having an increasingly difficult time defending the professor. "All right. I agree that he knows more than he's letting on, but we can still learn from him."

"So what do you think he's not telling?" asked Louis.

"Only everything," said Julie.

Peter hardly looked up from his journal. "Getting that crystal to my dad was sure important to him."

My dad... they all caught that.

"Sure," said Julie. "That was probably the only reason he told us anything at all."

"I don't think so," said Ben. "He wants to tell us more, but he can't."

"Geez, Ben." Julie grew more exasperated by the second. "We've run his little errand for him, he doesn't need us anymore, and now he's off to who-knows-where."

There was a long, uncomfortable silence. The only sound was that of Peter's pencil scratching across the thick, rough paper.

Over the last day, they had been thinking about the same thing, had been sorting and resorting what little they knew, and had been coming up with the same conclusion. No one had yet been willing to voice their thoughts aloud.

"Everyone knows about it," Louis finally said.

Peter stopped scribbling. The others looked at him. He looked up at Louis, then at the others.

"Everyone over thirty anyway," he mumbled.

Ben leaned forward, looked carefully at Peter and gave him a half nod. He turned to his sister.

"Remember when we asked Mom and Dad about Peter's father?"

"Sure. They didn't want to talk about it."

"I just figured they didn't want to talk about a messy marriage breakup."

"We know now that's not what happened." She perked up, began to show some interest in the direction that Ben was going. "Since they were hiding the reason behind John Murray's disappearance from us, and since we know that John Murray's disappearance has something to do with the gateway--"

Ben nodded sharply, "A plus B equals C, therefore A equals C and Mom and Dad know about the gateway."

"And if they know, and if the professor knows, then others in Ravenhill Court know."

"Like I said," Peter started scribbling in his journal again. "They all know. Everyone over thirty."

Julie sighed dejectedly. "But what is it they know—"

"—that we don't know," finished Louis.

Again there was only the scribbling of Peter's pencil as he drew in the journal. The others watched him as he worked, oblivious as to the attention being paid to him.

Julie looked up from Peter's journal. "You know what I think?" She pursed her lips and waited until she had everyone's attention; all but Peter's. "I think maybe Peter's father made that gate, and now he's stuck."

Peter had been paying attention after all. "Stuck where?"

"I'm not so sure that's it," said Louis. "I mean, that would make it important to Mr. Murray, but Ashton didn't look all that interested in bringing him back. There's something else going on."

"He's right," said Ben. "Ashton was real concerned about something, and it wasn't about bringing Peter's dad back from the other side."

"But he's still stuck," said Peter.

"But he was more concerned about some *others*. He said they would be lost if he didn't get the crystal."

"Now he has the crystal," said Peter.

Julie thought aloud, "And using it is dangerous."

"Looks like Ashton thinks so," said Ben. "I'll bet he's working for whoever controls the gate."

"That could be," agreed Julie. She leaned tiredly away from the table. "That still leaves the deep, dark secret of how this all came about to begin with."

"A deep, dark secret that this entire neighborhood is sittin' on."

Ben was sitting on the curb in front of his house, his feet resting on his red skateboard in front of him. The neighborhood was quiet on a warm afternoon. The last day of school. Summer was finally here.

Peter came out of his house and trudged slowly across the street. He dropped down beside Ben without a word.

For Peter, it had been a tough last couple of days at school. The incident the previous week had been only one more in a long line of incidents. A lot of people thought there might be something wrong with him.

"You all right?" asked Ben. He was staring down at his skateboard.

"Fine. I had to talk with some shrink for an hour."

"I heard."

"I think I have him convinced I'm a kid with abandonment issues."

Ben put on a fiendish grin. "You know…"

"I'm not adopted."

They sat quiet for a long time. The sun felt good. They knew that with school out of the way, they had all summer to devote to figuring out what was going on.

"I was thinking," Ben said finally.

"Let me know how that works for ya."

Ben let the skateboard roll back and forth under his feet. The metal wheels rumbled noisily across the asphalt.

"Twelve years," he said.

"What?"

"Ashton said twelve years. Your dad asked how long, and Ashton said *'twelve years on this side.'*"

"Yeah, that's right. My dad was real surprised… like maybe not that much time has gone by where he is."

Ben looked up from his skateboard at the neighborhood him. "So twelve years goes by here. Ashton, the professor, and who knows who else, are all waiting for the gateway to show up."

"The professor did say that he was expecting it."

"For a very long time…"

They fell silent again, and then Ben turned and gave Peter such a penetrating look that Peter began to squirm.

"Stop doing that."

"You, Peter… are connected somehow."

"Huh?"

"Your visions."

"What about 'em?" Peter asked defensively. "I've always had 'em."

"For about twelve years." Ben turned his attention back to his skateboard. "Kinda' weird."

Mike Margolis turned his car into Ravenhill Court and let it glide slowly up toward his house.

Up behind Ben and Peter, the garage door opened. Mr. Foster was going to spend what was left of the afternoon working on his old Mercury.

Adult Ben Foster was sitting on the curb in front of the old Foster house, the journal resting in his lap. He closed it and looked around at the abandoned neighborhood. The sky had grown gray with the oncoming dusk and shadows had started to finger their way amongst the empty houses.

He climbed to his feet and walked over to the old Mercury. His father's old Mercury. He brought a scruffy suitcase out of the trunk, slapped the trunk closed, and walked up the steep driveway to the house.

He put the suitcase down on the floor just inside the living room and set the journal on a side table. Dull light shone in from the large front window. He flipped the light switch on the wall and the lamp standing beside the couch turned on.

The house had power. That was good. The utility company had been there. *Weird.* He knew that he had contacted them, but he couldn't remember when. Things had been in a bit of turmoil lately.

He wandered down the hall and looked briefly in each of the rooms. Returning to the front of the house, Ben found himself standing in the kitchen, staring at the metal-legged table with a sense of melancholy.

He went back into the living room and picked up the journal. He sat down in his father's old easy chair and laid the book in his lap.

Chapter Seven

The Foster's garage door was open, as was usually the case on Saturdays. The old Mercury took up the right half of the garage. Mr. Foster was tinkering around under the hood, and young Ben was leaning on the fender, his back against the car.

"Dad..."

"Yeah, Ben." Mr. Foster reached an arm out and picked up a wrench without lifting himself from under the hood.

"What did Mr. Murray do?"

"Waddya mean, 'what did he do'?"

"For a living. What kind of work did he do?"

There was a slight pause. Ben could tell that his dad had stopped whatever he was doing in there.

"Why?" Mr. Foster finally asked. The tinkering under hood started up again.

"Just curious."

Mr. Foster didn't answer right away. There was the dull clinking of metal against cast iron.

"Scientific research. Smart man, John Murray."

Ben turned about at that and leaned forward over the fender. There was the hint of rising excitement in his voice. "Research? Really? Like what?"

"Couldn't say." Mr. Foster glanced up briefly, looked directly at Ben, then returned to the shadows of the engine compartment. "Secretive lot, that bunch."

"Yeah?"

Mr. Foster glanced up again, and again only briefly.

"Very."

Ben, Julie and Louis were sitting about the table in the fort. Peter was out of sight, sitting up in the tower. They had gone nowhere in solving the mystery, lately only coming up with more questions. There was a growing sense of frustration.

Ben was impatient. "We're going to have to go back to the ravine."

"What good would that do?" groaned Julie.

Peter called down from the tower. "The gateway is closed."

"Yeah... it was closed before," said Ben. "But it opened."

"Doesn't mean it will again," said Julie.

"That's true." Louis straightened and nodded sharply.

"It wouldn't hurt to go back," said Ben.

"That's true, too," nodded Louis.

"What about the professor?" asked Peter. The others could hear him moving about. He was positioning himself to come down from the tower.

"What about him?" asked Ben.

Julie's face twisted and she almost growled. "You mean other than the fact that he's gone? That he took our number and split?"

Peter was halfway down the ladder. He stepped from the last rung. "Secret code..."

"That he tried to make out meant nothing."

Louis gave yet another sharp nod. "That is certainly true."

Julie turned a deadly eye to Louis. "Stop doing that."

Ben was staring down at the table in front of him. He had been listening to the banter back and forth, and it was the same conversation they always had. There wasn't enough new information coming in.

"We're talking in circles," he said softly, but the frustration was as evident as ever. "We've done good, we know a lot more than we did, but without more *intel*, we're not going any further with this." He lifted his gaze from the surface of the table and up to the faces of the others. "We have two sources to get more: the professor, and the ravine."

The room was painfully quiet for several moments before Julie spoke up.

"There's the government spook," she offered.

"Yeah..." Ben mumbled patiently. "Yeah, there's Ashton. But how would we find him?"

Julie started to answer, then stopped herself, scrunched up her face and nodded silently.

Louis, however, was willing to respond. "By way of the ravine and the gateway, or through the Prof."

"Like I said. Two sources."

"Well... I've said it all along," said Julie, folding her arms. "The professor needs to spill what he knows."

◊ ◊ ◊

Louis stood on the sidewalk outside the Foster house. Sunday was looking like it would shape up to be a pleasant early summer day. The sun was out and already working to burn off the coastal fog. Up the street, Mr. Addison was dragging his garden hose out, holding a sprinkler with his free hand.

But not all was pleasant.

Across the street, Donna Osborne came around her from her side yard and walked across her front lawn. She gave Louis a dark look before stepping up onto her porch.

Louis turned toward the intersection when he heard voices.

Tony Margolis and his toady Danny Bigalow were starting across the street, coming right toward Louis. As they came nearer, Danny's grin grew.

Tony's expression look much more threatening.

"Who let you out, Bennett?" he sneered.

"No one." Louis knew there was no way to win this thing. For now, he wanted to wait to see which way the confrontation would go in order to decide which way to turn. Still, his response was way too weak and he knew it. He hadn't been on his toes; his mistake for letting the nice morning distract him.

Tony stepped up to within a few inches of Louis, glared down at him. Tony was big for his age, which was three years older than Louis, and Louis was small for his.

"Then you shouldn't be out, should ya', boy?"

Danny stood beside Tony, sneering and bubbling with pleasure.

Tony's smile sent a cold finger down Louis' spine. "You lookin' maybe to rob somebody?"

"No," said Louis flatly.

Tony glanced behind Louis, up at the Foster's open garage.

"I think maybe ya' are. I think maybe you're lookin' to rip off the Fosters."

"Yeah," Danny could hardly restrain himself. "That's what I think."

"Ben's my friend," said Louis.

"Friend?" Tony feigned shock and surprise. "Friend? You got friends?"

"I have lots of friends."

Tony moved up quickly, even before Louis could finish the statement. His body pushed against Louis. The words came colder now. "Not here, you don't, boy. Maybe you're thinking of someplace else."

"Yeah." Danny moved in closer.

"That right?" There was a sparkle in Tony's glare. "You thinkin' someplace else?"

"Yeah," Danny said eagerly. "Like Africa!"

Louis stood frozen in place.

A car turned off Edgewood and into Ravenhill Court. Louis kept his eyes fixed on Tony. They could hear the car come to an easy stop behind Tony and Danny.

Danny turned to see who it was, then quickly turned back and looked up at Tony. He spoke low and soft and somewhat urgently.

"It's Mike," he said.

Tony slowly eased back from Louis. He turned and looked behind him at his big brother. He still wore the dark, angry look, and it was clear that he wasn't happy at having his fun interrupted.

Mike Margolis gave Tony a long, very definitive stare from his position behind the steering wheel of his Chevy.

Tony finally backed down. He turned and gave Louis a hard shove.

"This ain't done," he said abruptly and stalked off. Danny Bigalow glared back at Louis as he quickly followed after Tony.

Mike Margolis gave Louis only a quick glance, revealing nothing, before letting his foot off the brake and coasting his car up into the court.

Ben came up behind Louis from the direction of his house.

"What was that about?"

"Nothing," Louis said sharply.

"Nothing my Aunt Bessie's behind."

Louis was still trying to get over the shakes. He shoved his hands into his pants pockets. "Same ol', same ol'."

Ben could still see the receding figures of Tony and Danny. He knew from personal experience what they could be like. He also had a pretty good idea how they would work on Louis.

"You say so," he said.

"I say so."

The sound of a screen door slapping shut broke through the Sunday morning silence. Across the street, Peter was coming across his yard. He started across the street toward them.

Julie came out of the Foster garage. She called down to the others long before reaching them.

"What's everybody standin' around for? Let's do this."

The four of them started up into the court. Ahead of them on the right, Mike Margolis was walking around to the front of his car. He lifted the hood to have a look at the idling engine.

Up on the left, almost opposite the Margolis', stood the LaMothe house. A covered deck ran the width of the house. They reached the wooden steps, climbed up onto the deck, and Julie reached out and knocked.

They waited in silence. When no one answered, Julie knocked again.

"Maybe she's not home," said Peter.

"Where would she go?" asked Julie. "I don't think she's left the house since she retired."

"What did she do?" asked Louis.

The others looked at him curiously.

"She was the principle at the school," said Julie.

"Our school?"

"Yeah, Louis... our school... big building with desks..."

"It was awful," grumbled Peter.

"She wasn't that bad," said Ben, grinning broadly.

Julie could only half agree. "Far as principles go."

The front door opened then and all four were immediately silent. Mrs. LaMothe stared haughtily down at them. It was several seconds before she said anything.

"I believe I advised you yesterday that the Professor was not available."

"Yes ma'am," said Ben. "But... we were hoping you could tell us where he went--"

"And when we might expect his return," finished Julie.

It didn't appear as though Mrs. LaMothe was going to respond to this. She said nothing for a long time, continued to look down the bridge of her long nose at them.

Louis and Peter grew nervous.

Ben waited expectantly.

Julie just waited.

"The Professor's date of return is not known," said Mrs. LaMothe at last. There was another very long pause. "Was there something else?"

Julie started to say something, but Ben cut her off.

"No ma'am," he jumped in. "Thank you for your time, Mrs. LaMothe."

Ben turned away, and Louis and Peter quickly stepped off the porch ahead of him.

Julie stared silently up into the steady gaze of Mrs. LaMothe. She wasn't about to let this old school principle psych her out.

Ben, still on the deck, looked back over his shoulder. "Julie?" he urged.

Julie smiled thinly at Mrs. LaMothe, but said nothing.

Mrs. LaMothe gave the girl a dismissive nod. "Miss Foster," she said officiously.

"Thank you, Mrs. LaMothe." Julie turned around and she and Ben stepped down from the deck together. "So much for that," she said to Ben. "I guess we take a hike."

Several hours later, they found themselves in the clearing in the ravine. The four of them were kneeling around a small fire pit they had put together in one corner. Ben was trying to get a fire going using the kindling they had gathered together into a small pile within the circle of stones.

There was no sign of the gateway and the clearing was thick with shadows.

"LaMothe is on no business trip," Julie grumbled loudly.

"Julie... obvious," said Ben.

"Where would he go?" asked Peter.

"Wherever those numbers we gave him sent him," said Julie.

"And just where would that be?"

"How would I know?"

"What do you do with a number?" asked Louis. "It isn't like it's a locker number in some bus terminal."

"How do you know that?" Julie asked sharply, sending Louis back into silence.

Ben sat back and watched the small fire come to life. "Because, Julie, it is very unlikely that Peter's father would reach out from some alternate universe and give us the number of a locker in a bus terminal."

The four of them were startled at the sound of Ashton's voice.

"It's not an alternate universe," he said calmly. He stood behind them, near the heart of the clearing. He had come alone. He was looking to where the gateway had made its last appearance. "John is in, shall we say... the universe."

They were all standing now, Julie's stance more defiant than the others. "If it's different than ours, doesn't that make it alternate?"

"I'm afraid not."

"That doesn't make any sense."

"Therein lies part of the problem."

"What problem?"

Ashton strolled toward the group until he was standing before the slowly growing campfire. The others eyed him suspiciously, following his movements.

Ben echoed Julie's question. "What problem?"

Ashton spoke without looking directly at anyone. "John was conducting some rather unique experiments for our organization."

"We get that," said Julie. "And something went wrong."

"You might say that," Ashton smiled thinly, gave a slight, sardonic chuckle.

"I would be more interested in hearing what <u>you</u> have to say."

"I suppose you would." Ashton looked at Julie for a few moments, glanced at the others, finally turned his back to them and indicated the clearing they were in. "Look around you. Look at the clearing we're in. The rock walls. The fire at your feet."

"Yeah..." Julie urged cautiously.

Ashton turned again, slowly about, and looked directly at the group of young people. "Nothing that I'm looking at is real. This place... doesn't exist. It's a figment. It's all illusion. Everything. Those that were caught up in John Murray's experiment... they were caught up in this fabrication."

They stared at Ashton in open confusion.

"I don't understand," mumbled Ben.

"I would be very surprised if you did, young man." Ashton grew thoughtful, turned introspective. "So... they bring in the cavalry. That's me." He looked upward as if taking in the world around them. "Look where I end up."

Everyone was very quiet for a long time. None of what Ashton had said made any kind of sense, so what was there to say? How could they respond? What was there to ask?

As for Ashton, he had apparently said all that he was going to say on the matter, whatever the matter was. He wasn't likely to give them answers, only more questions.

Peter finally broke the awkward silence.

"This is way too weird. You are way too weird."

This took Ben off guard, but he had to agree. "And that's saying something, coming from Peter."

Ashton smiled sadly at them both.

"More so than you realize." He turned and looked again at the heart of the clearing. "I can guarantee you that John will not be making an appearance here today."

"Is that right?" Julie was eager to get back into the conversation. "We don't really know what your guarantees are worth, though, do we, Mr. Ashton?"

Ashton didn't really care. He gave a half shrug as he turned to leave. There was a tiredness to his gesture and his tone of voice.

"As you wish, Miss Foster." He started toward the opening that would take him back down the ravine. "I would suggest that you leave in time to get home before nightfall. I know I wouldn't want to be traipsing in this brush in the dark."

Mr. and Mrs. Foster were sitting in the darkened living room watching television. The only sound was that of the television program coming through the small speakers. The flickering of the black and white screen created shadows and light that danced across the walls of the room.

Ben and Julie came in through the back door at the far end of the hall. Julie turned and went into her bedroom, and Ben continued on alone. He stopped just before coming into the living room and silently observed his parents.

The flickering of the television screen sent light and shadows across their faces, just as it did the walls of the room. They both seemed to be entranced by the show.

After a few moments, though, Dad turned his head and looked over at Ben. It was a perceptive gaze, as if he... *understood.*

He said nothing. His expression changed little. He turned his attention slowly back to the television.

Ben continued to stand there, just inside the darkened hall, silently observing his parents, as if seeing them for the first time. It was as though, if he watched them long enough, the secret might be revealed to him.

That he, too, would understand.

Chapter Eight

Peter sat writing single-mindedly in his journal, as he most always did now whenever they were in the fort. He pretty much ignored the somewhat heated conversation that Ben and Julie were having.

"I don't buy it," said Ben.

"It makes a kind of sense," said Julie.

"Sense? Sense? It doesn't make any sense. What does *'none of it is real'* mean? That's crazier than anything Peter's ever said."

Julie's expression grew a hint darker. "And yet you believe Peter..."

Ben was suddenly flustered, and it took him a moment to recover. When he spoke again, his words were soft and precise.

"Ashton is not Peter."

"Then you explain what's going on."

They both involuntarily sucked in a frantic breath at the sound of angry voices coming from outside. A second later, Julie rushed toward the ladder to the tower and Ben slid down the bench to the wall beside the front door. He peered through a narrow crack between the boards.

Peter looked calmly up from his journal, but said nothing. He didn't seem to be affected by the activity around him. He seemed almost apart from it.

Julie was already scrambling back down from the tower.

"They got Louis," she whispered harshly.

Ben could see Tony forcibly pushing Louis toward the fort, Danny trailing behind them along the very narrow trail running from the main trail up to the fort.

When the got to the fort, Tony reached around Louis and banged on the wall beside the door.

"Open up!"

When the door didn't immediately open, Tony leaned up close to the wall and his voice became a low, menacing whisper.

"How 'bout I hurt your boy?"

"Waddya want, Tony?"

"You deaf as well as dumb, Foster? I told ya' what I want." Tony yelled out loud and harsh, "Open the door!"

Ben looked anxiously over at Julie. Ben didn't frighten easily, but he also really didn't like not being in control of the situation. This was one more in a long line of uncontrollable situations that had come up the last few weeks.

Julie nodded curtly. Open the door. What else was there to do?

Ben slid the latch aside. The door burst open as Tony shoved Louis in ahead of him before pushing his own way in. He moved around the table and slid in on the bench.

"So," he said. He looked content. "What do we have here?"

Danny stepped in and closed the door.

"Playing house, huh?" His words were almost giggles.

Tony liked the suggestion. He eyed Julie. "Now that has possibilities."

"Dream on," said Julie.

Tony sighed tritely, looked at the others in the room. Louis had moved over beside Julie, near the tower ladder. Peter stood in one corner.

Tony looked sharply at Ben, who was sitting at the table opposite him. He jabbed a thumb in Louis' direction.

"I wanted to warn you about that one there. He's been casing out the neighborhood." Tony gave Julie another once-over. "Who knows what else?"

"You're a pig," Julie said with a disgusted sneer.

Danny made snorting sounds.

Tony smiled thinly. "Gotta protect our own, Miss Julie."

Ben spoke softly, so that everyone was forced to stop and listen more closely.

"On that we agree."

"Ohhhh," Tony's smile broadened. "Is that a threat, Foster?"

Ben didn't respond. The calm expression on his face remained unchanged.

Tony decided to move on. He leaned back and studied the room again.

"Not a bad setup," he said appreciatively. "A few changes, I do believe I could feel right at home here."

"Yeah," Danny bubbled.

"I'd burn it down first," said Ben.

Tony finally lost his sense of humor. His tone turned dangerous. He leaned forward.

"I don't think you appreciate the seriousness of your situation, Foster. This party has the potential of going any number of ways. Most of 'em are painful."

"You don't frighten me," said Ben.

Over in the corner, Peter had a blank stare. His skin had turned pasty.

Something wasn't quite right...

Tony leaned even closer to Ben, now halfway over the table.

"Really? I think I..." He sniffed at the air. "Yes... I smell *fear* in the air."

Ben leaned the rest of the way over the table until the two of them were almost nose to nose.

"I think it's crap you smell. Not surprising. Your mouth is right under your nose."

Tony started to rise up in anger. But halfway to his feet his expression changed. His movement unexpectedly slowed.

In the corner of the room, the blank expression on Peter's face had turned glassy.

Tony rose slowly up the rest of the way to his feet. He gazed at Ben with a look of confusion.

Something wasn't quite right...

Ben stared back at Tony, somewhat bewildered.

He looked over at Julie. *What the heck's going on?*

In response, Julie contorted her face. *I don't know.*

Ben turned back to Tony. "Uh... heh? Tony?"

Tony twisted his head mechanically to the left, then to the right. He frowned.

His facial muscles suddenly relaxed. He turned and started toward the door. Danny stepped aside to let him pass. He started to say something to Tony, but before he had a chance, his own expression turned to a dull emptiness.

Tony opened the door and stepped outside.

Danny looked at the group in the fort, but there wasn't anything behind the eyes. He turned and followed Tony out the door.

Julie immediately jumped up onto the wooden ladder and was up inside the tower in seconds. Looking through the slatted opening, she watched Tony and Danny as they stepped from the side trail and out onto the main trail.

The moment they were on the main trail, they began talking.

Something isn't right...

It took Julie a few moments before she realized...

Tony and Danny were repeating their conversation from days earlier... *word for word...*

Tony Margolis was walking confidently along the trail, with Danny Bigalow following along beside him.

"...and Miss Harris sent him to the principal," said Danny. He had a huge, rat grin on his face. "And Walker sent him to the nurse. And he was supposed to see the dean after school, but guess what... He didn't show up."

Tony Margolis listened quietly to the kid's unbounded glee.

"Man, oh man," said Danny. "It was so boss."

They reached the point in the trail where the hidden path forked off and led to the fort. They continued past along the main trail.

"What did he mean?" asked Tony.

"Don't know. Maybe he told Walker." Danny bubbled with joy. "He is so weird."

Tony spoke as if to himself, "He is a strange little creep, all right."

Julie climbed down out of the tower.

"You are not going to believe this--" She stopped when she saw the way Ben was silently watching Peter.

Peter had returned to the table. He had his journal out and was contentedly writing. He was either ignoring or was unaware of all that had just happened.

"What's going on?" she whispered, then looked around the room. Her head was swimming. "Where's Louis?"

There was only Ben and Julie... and Peter hunched over his journal.

Chapter Nine

The Foster family sat around the dinner table, which was the breakfast table with a table cloth thrown over it. There was an uncomfortable silence in the room.

Mrs. Foster set down her fork, took a drink of milk, then carefully set down the glass.

"I understand that Professor LaMothe has returned from his business trip," she said. She picked up her fork and took another bite of her dinner.

Mr. Foster responded without look up from his meal. "Is that so?"

"So I understand."

The exchange was stilted and forced. Ben and Julie looked at each other with barely hidden skepticism.

"What kind of business?" asked Ben.

Both parents looked confused.

"Just... business." Mrs. Foster held her fork out over her plate. "What does it matter?"

Mr. Foster thought he had the answer. "The professor has involved himself in a number of business interests since retiring."

Ben nodded, as if he might half believe that if he would just give himself a chance; which he wouldn't.

Julie returned to eating, almost as mechanically as the conversation she was witnessing. She spoke up without looking up from her food.

"Do you know Mr. Ashton?" she asked.

Ben watched Dad.

Dad considered the question thoughtfully. "I... don't believe so. Why do you ask?"

"Just someone we ran into."

"At school?"

"He knows John Murray," said Ben, deflecting the question. He thought it was a reasonable answer, and hoped that his father's response might provide some insight.

Dad smiled confidently. "Ah... *that* crowd."

"Weird guy" said Julie. "Weirder ideas."

"Being a part of that bunch, I wouldn't doubt it."

"So, you've never heard of him, then?" asked Ben.

"Can't say as I have," Dad sighed. "But then, I didn't move in the same circles as John."

Ben was sitting at the table in the fort, Peter's journal lay opened in front of him. The light coming in through the small windows was enough to read by.

On the first page was an overhead sketch of Ravenhill Court, showing the nine homes, each one labeled with the family's name.

The next few pages had drawings of some of the locations around Ravenhill, these too carefully labeled. There was Blue Clay Ravine, Ravenhill Ridge, Pirate's Cove...

The next pages showed drawings of the people living in Ravenhill Court. Peter was very good, and even without the names that he had meticulously printed beneath each picture, Ben easily recognized everyone.

Ben turned the page again and began reading of Peter's recent experiences, or more precisely about their experiences as seen through Peter's eyes. He skimmed these quickly, feeling a bit guilty about sneaking a look at the journal without asking. But it was important that he find out what was going on in Peter's head.

He stopped at an odd passage and read more slowly, more carefully:

> The laboratory was a large room, the walls lined with counters and glass-faced cabinets. There was a shelf rack filled with metal boxes fronted with levers, dials and buttons.

Ben felt a cold, tingling sensation spread throughout his entire body. *What laboratory?*

> Cables ran from the machine rack to a tall, rectangular framework the size and shape of a large doorway.

There was a panicked banging on the door and Ben nearly fell back off the bench and onto the floor.

Julie called out loud and desperate. "Ben! Ben! Open up!"

Ben hurried to the door and slid the latch aside. Julie reached in and grabbed Ben's arm even before the door was fully open.

"You gotta come!" She pulled at him. "Now. There's a spy sedan outside Peter's house."

"A what?"

"A shiny black car. Come on!"

Ben had to struggle to turn and get the door closed and locked before Julie had him scrambling down the trail.

They stumbled out into the street, coming from between the Margolis and Addison houses.

Peter was being led across his front yard toward a black sedan that was parked in the street in front of his house. The uniformed figures on either side of Peter were the associates that had been with Ashton at the ravine.

Ashton was speaking with Mrs. Murray on the porch. They appeared to be in calm conversation. She had her arms wrapped around herself, a cigarette held between her fingers.

Once they finished their exchange, Ashton placed a comforting hand on Mrs. Murray's arm, stepped off the porch and walked toward the car, following Peter.

Peter stopped beside the waiting car and looked up into the court. He had to have seen Ben and Julie, but gave no sign. A moment later he climbed into the back seat of the vehicle.

Ashton, one hand now on the roof of the sedan, heard the pounding footsteps, looked up and saw Ben and Julie running down the street toward him. Without acknowledging them, he climbed into the back seat beside Peter, and the vehicle pulled away from the curb.

Ben and Julie, still rushing headlong in the direction of the black sedan, slowly heading out of the cul-de-sac, come to a stumbling, faltering stop.

They tried to catch their breath.

"Great..." said Ben, sucking in air, "Just great... what now?"

Julie nudged Ben with her elbow. She was looking back behind them, in the direction of the LaMothe house.

"Maybe he can tell us," she said.

Professor LaMothe was standing in front of his house. He wasn't looking at the activity going on down the street at the Murray's. He was watching Ben and Julie.

He turned about and walked back to his house, took the front steps one at a time. By the time he reached the large chair at the far end of the deck, Ben was at the steps, and Julie was right behind him.

Ben sat in the small deck chair near the Professor, but Julie chose to stand near the railing, arms folded. Her gaze was sharp and accusatory, as was her stance.

She let Ben talk first.

"What are they doing with Peter, Professor?" he asked. "Where are they taking him?"

The professor put on his most thoughtful face.

"How long have you known Louis, Ben?"

Ben and Julie both looked taken aback.

"Wha-- uh... I don't know... a while."

"What does that have to do with Peter?" asked Julie.

"Please," the Professor said gently. "You've known Louis for... *a while*, you say."

"Yeah. He's in my class."

The professor nodded sagely."And... his family lives in a house just outside the Court."

"Yeah, that's right. On the corner, across the street."

"Do either of you happen to remember when they moved into the house?"

Ben looked over at Julie. The two appeared to be trying to draw an answer from one another; unsuccessfully. Julie looked away from Ben then and turned a piercing glare on the professor.

"What is this about, Professor?"

"We'll get there, Julie. I promise." The professor spoke again to them both. "Do you recall the Bennett family moving in?"

"I don't know," said Ben. "I think so. I guess it had to have been a long time ago."

"In point of fact," said the professor, "it was a few days ago."

"Professor—" Julie grumbled.

"That's crazy," said Ben. "He's been in my class for, geez... for as long as I can remember."

"Louis Bennett has never been in your class."

Ben and Julie squirmed uncomfortably.

Something is very, very wrong...

"But we've know Louis for," Julie struggled to remember. "For... *always*."

There was a moment of heavy silence, and then the professor leaned forward and spoke into that silence.

"You saw Louis for the first time in the clearing while on your way to the ravine in which you found the gateway."

"But I know him," Ben said pleadingly.

"Ben... Ben, listen to me. Prior to that encounter... Louis did not exist."

The hint of fear washed across Ben's face. Julie wrapped her arms around herself and took hold, as if to keep herself from fading away. It felt as though their world was turning into mist around them.

"I created him," the professor continued. "I created a fellow traveler, with all the complex issues and problems arising from within this time and place in our history."

"Are you... what Ashton told us..." Ben wasn't sure he wanted to know the answer. "It's true?"

"That would depend entirely on what Mr. Ashton told you."

Julie spoke in a faint whisper. "None of this is real," she said.

The professor leaned back in his chair. He looked at the young people standing in front of him as if examining them for flaws. He turned his attention then out beyond his covered deck, took in the quiet scene of the neighborhood. When he finally responded, his voice was calm and the tone was cool and low.

"Not the school that you attend, not the jobs that your parents go to each morning. Not that hint of the ocean that I smell in the air."

"That's not possible," said Ben.

"The world, and all that is taking place in the world, is illusion."

"How?"

"What does it mean?" asked Julie.

The professor continued to focus his attention on the neighborhood. "Nothing outside the Court is happening beyond the minds and imaginations of the adults in Ravenhill Court. People and places and things exist only during the moments when someone in Ravenhill Court is thinking of them."

"That..." Julie struggled to wrap her mind around it. "That sounds a lot like a dream."

The professor looked up into Julie's face and smiled, albeit sadly. "That's right. That's exactly right, dear girl. We are living in a dream."

Ben stepped out into the street. Behind him, on the lawn in front of the professor's deck, stood Julie and the Professor. Neither of them spoke. They watched Ben in silence, motionless.

Ben studied the neighborhood that was spread out before him, seemingly looking for something, anything, that would tell him for sure that none of what the professor had said was true.

Throughout Ravenhill Court, all had returned to normalcy. It was a bright, clear day.

Mrs. Murray was going back inside.

The garage door to the Foster house was open and Ben saw his dad walk around behind the old Mercury before stepping back into the shadow of the garage.

At the Margolis house, Mike climbed into his fifties Chevy. He backed it out onto the street and drove slowly toward the intersection at the entrance of the Court.

Naturally, Donna was waiting on the curb in front of her house. She waved joyfully at Mike as he passed. He ignored her, as always. Naturally...

Mr. Addison was kneeling beside his lawn mower, giving it a good going over before starting in up. Mr. Addison always seemed to be mowing his yard.

Professor LaMothe stepped up beside Ben.

"It's true," said Ben, barely above a whisper.

"Yes."

"But it's more than that. It's more than what you've told us. Isn't it?"

The professor answered hesitantly.

"I'm afraid so."

Chapter Ten

Looking up from the journal, the middle-aged Ben Foster saw that the sun had set and the evening beyond the front window was a dull, faded gray.

He set the journal aside and stood up. His body was more than half a century old and he could feel every day of it in his bones. He carefully stretched as he walked across the living room and stood at the large window that looked out on the neighborhood of Ravenhill Court.

Two people were sitting on the curb in front of the Foster house, their backs to Ben Foster. From behind, even in the gloomy dusk, Ben could see that they were both about his age; one was a woman with long brown hair, the other a black man.

Ben stepped out the front door and walked down the lawn. He sat beside them on the curb.

"Hey, Julie."

"Hey, Ben," she answered. There was a tinge of sadness in her voice. "Long time, huh?"

"Looks that way." Ben leaned forward and looked across at Louis. "Louis. A bit surprised to see you."

"Can't keep a good man down," said Louis. "I don't get this."

"Yeah... that's right. Crazy if you did. You weren't around for the last of it." Ben nodded at his sister. "Julie gettin' you caught up?"

"Enough to confuse me," said Louis. "We were created? We were part of a dream?"

Julie smiled grimly. "Only the adults in Ravenhill Court were real."

"And Peter," Ben corrected.

"Yes," said Julie. "And Peter."

Louis had a bit of a revelation. "His visions..."

Julie gave another thin smile in answer, but said nothing. Ben nodded once, and then again, but said nothing.

Louis continued to struggle to process it all. After a few moments, he indicated the abandoned neighborhood that they found themselves in.

"But what about--"

"They went home," said Julie, cutting him off.

"Home?"

"To the waking world. And we... we came here."

"Okay..." Louis still didn't have a firm grasp on it all. "So... and just where is here?"

"A generated universe," said Ben. "The world of the dream bubble that we had been living in before... sort of... not quite. All the same bits and pieces, put together by John Murray, to give us, the children of Ravenhill Court, a place to live out our lives." Ben leaned forward and slowly stood up. "What say we go inside?"

Ben led them up to the house and inside. Once in the living room, Ben silently beckoned them in. Julie smiled nostalgically as she stepped into the center of the room.

"It's smaller than I remember."

"That's what they say about going home again," said Ben.

Louis moved over to the large picture window and looked out on the neighborhood. Ben stepped up beside him.

"You okay?" he asked.

It was several seconds before Louis could respond.

"I don't think so."

Young Ben and Julie followed the same trail they had travelled on their two previous trips to the ravine. They reached the fork in the trail where they had first seen Ashton. The left fork would eventually take them to the ravine; the right fork would take them to wherever Ashton had come from.

Ben started up the right fork without slowing his steady pace. Julie followed silently behind him. After a few dozen yards, they came to wooden steps set into a steep hillside. A rickety wooden rail ran along the left side of the staircase.

At the top of the steps, they came out onto a clearing of dirt and dry grass. A dirt road emptied into the clearing from the right, and there was a worn tire path running from the road up to steel double doors, twelve feet high and ten feet wide, that were set into the hillside on the other side of the landing.

One of the doors stood ajar. Ben and Julie approached and Ben peered into the dark cavern.

"See anything?" asked Julie.

"Dark," said Ben. After only a moment's hesitation, he slipped inside. Again, Julie was right behind him.

The empty hall was fourteen feet wide, eighteen feet high, and extended into the mountain as far as they could see. It wasn't completely dark. There were small light fixtures hanging on the walls on either side about twelve feet up and spaced out every dozen paces. These provided just enough illumination to create shadows.

The massive room was empty. If not for the faintly glowing lamps, the place would seem to be abandoned. The floor and walls were made of concrete, and as Ben and Julie walked down the great tunnel, their footsteps echoed hollowly out into the darkness.

They saw a pair of lights hanging on the left wall in the distance, set lower than the other fixtures. As they came nearer, they saw that the fixtures were set to either side of a standard sized door.

Standing directly before it, Ben looked questioningly at Julie.

Julie shrugged a shoulder despondently. "What do we have to lose?"

With that, Ben reached out and took hold of the knob. It turned easily and he opened the door.

The long, narrow hallway was lit with fluorescent lights. Doors were set every sixteen feet, each inset with frosted glass panels.

Ashton was standing at the third door down, looking in their direction. He didn't seem at all surprised to see them. He gave a beckoning wave before disappearing through the door.

What do we have to lose?

Ben and Julie started down the hall. Reaching the door, Ben paused long enough to take an extra breath, but so long enough that he might change his mind, before stepping through.

The laboratory was a large room. The walls were lined with counters and glass-faced cabinets. Drafting tables and more counters were scattered haphazardly around the room. Lamps and fixtures were set in strategic locations, offering plenty of light at their target locations but creating moving shadows.

The men who had escorted Ashton to the ravine days before were standing amidst the tables and counters. They watched silently as the two young people came further into the room.

"This is what Peter wrote about," Ben said softly. He moved into an open area beyond the counters. An electric generator was visible through an open doorway in a far wall. Cables ran from the other room into the laboratory and up to a shelf rack of metal boxes fronted with levers, dials and buttons. More cables ran from the machine rack over to a tall, rectangular framework the size and shape of a large doorway.

Several floor fans labored to cool the room, but at best were only managing to keep the air circulated.

Ashton stood in the center of the open area. Peter was standing beside him.

Julie stepped up beside Ben.

"Holy cow," she said.

"You said it."

Ashton half turned and looked at Ben, then looked to the shadows beyond, in the direction of the main door. He spoke to someone behind Ben and Julie.

"Their presence here must be your doing," he said.

Ben and Julie turned and saw Professor LaMothe standing just inside the doorway. He started across the room.

"I thought it only fair they be here for this," he said.

"How much do they know?"

"Not much beyond what you told them." The professor reached the center of the open area. He studied the gateway apparatus, and after a long time nodded in a begrudging sign of approval.

"Not bad," he said. "Considering you scratched it together with nothing but sixties tech."

"It should do the job," said Ashton.

He looked over at one of his assistants and nodded. The assistant went into the other room and started the generator. The sound threatened to drown out all other sound in the room until he pulled the door closed. A corner of the door had been cut away in order to allow the cabling to come through. This, like everything else, had the appearance of being makeshift.

Julie leaned close to Ben and whispered harshly. "You see? The professor is with them. Ben, we've been had."

Ben looked sharply at the professor. "What's going on, Professor?"

"Everything is going to be all right, son."

Ashton watched the assistant walk over to the machine rack, then looked over at Ben.

"We're going to try it your way, young man," he said, then turned an intense eye to the professor. "But hang onto your hat,

LaMothe. If it doesn't work, we're committed. The bubble will collapse."

"Of course." Professor LaMothe nodded his head in slow agreement.

With that, Ashton turned again to his assistant standing in front of the equipment rack.

"Do it," he said.

The man turned and reached for the first dial. He slowly turned it the number "6". One band encircling the opening in the gateway brightened as power began to surge through it. He reached then for the second dial, calmly turned it to the "3".

The second band encircling the opening in the gateway apparatus sparked and sputtered as power surged through.

"So," said Julie, "Now we know what the numbers mean."

Professor LaMothe spoke quietly to Ben and Julie as he calmly watched the assistant move over to the third and final dial.

"John Murray has been attempting to build a permanent bridge between the waking world and the dream world in which we find ourselves."

The man at the equipment rack turned the third dial to "6". The third band encircling the gateway apparatus brightened as power surged through it.

The professor struggled to maintain a sense of calm. "There are two critical components to accomplishing this bridge," he said. "The first is to synchronize the portal on the outside with this one inside the bubble."

"But Professor," Ben looked confused. "If none of this is real, then this gateway isn't real. How can he create a bridge between a real gateway and one that isn't real?"

The professor smiled approvingly and lifted a finger. "Ah... therein lies the second critical component."

"The crystal," said Julie.

"The crystal," said the professor.

"But that's not real, either," said Ben.

"The crystal was a virtual representation of the data that comprises this dream bubble."

"I don't get it."

"The bubble is a collection of thousands of trillions of bits of information, a copy of which was contained in the data crystal. When Peter handed it to his father, and John carried it back across the portal threshold, the virtual essence of the crystal was lost, but the data within it was ascertained by John's equipment."

◊ ◊ ◊

Adult Ben Foster was sitting in his father's old easy chair, a thermos cup held in one hand. He leaned forward and handed the thermos bottle and a large ceramic cup to Julie. He slid back in the chair then, took a sip of coffee and looked over at Louis.

"Peter's father was conducting shared dream experiments when something unexpected happened," said Ben. "A fully realized dream bubble formed. That's what they called it. A 'dream bubble'."

"I'm with you," said Louis, "sort of."

"Very exciting at first, this virtual world. Those within it living lives and the world going along its very merry way. Then, somehow, I don't know the details, John Murray got pulled out of our happy little existence. This created a cascade effect of problems back in the real world, and those involved in the dream experiment were trapped here."

Julie set her coffee mug down on the arm of the couch. "Life continued on in Ravenhill Court."

"While back in the real world, John Murray frantically sought a solution."

"Remember," said Julie. "Time passes at a different speed here than in the waking world."

"Which compounded the problem," said Ben, shifting forward in his chair, and made certain that Louis was paying attention. "For you see, the primary dreamer, the person through which the dream bubble was formed, was Peter."

"And back in the real world," said Julie, "Peter was only a baby."

Louis, who had begun to think he might be getting a handle on this, was visibly shaken. "How could a baby create a world like Ravenhill Court? And everything else?"

"Peter was the channel," said Ben. "The contents of the bubble were generated collectively by all the members of the dream experiment."

Julie waited until Louis had a few moments to let all this sink in, then she slid forward until she was sitting on the edge of the couch. She spoke to both Louis and her brother.

"You know the bizarre thing? We really don't know how true to life any of what we experienced was."

"Our entire universe was just a dream," Ben agreed.

"Our universe was an accident."

◊ ◊ ◊

Ashton gave his assistant a silent signal. The man lifted a wide-handled lever.

A spiderweb of electricity materialized within the opening of the gateway apparatus. A moment later, the portal opened and the entire room glowed a bright, clear blue, the blue emanating from within the gateway.

The room on the other side of the portal was filled with very advanced equipment, all high tech, all highly polished.

John Murray stepped into view.

Ashton stepped directly in front of the gateway. "All right, John," he said. "Good luck to you."

"Appreciate it." John looked beyond Ashton at the others in the laboratory. "Good to see you, Professor."

"John," the professor gave a slight bow.

John smiled at Peter. "Hey, kiddo." With that, he stepped to one side and began working at a computer that was sitting on a counter.

"Initiating," he said. Everyone was silent, anxiously watching John work on the other side of the portal. "Engaging."

The room on the other side went very white, then glowed a bright blue.

"All right," said John. "Beginning synchronization."

The images within the gateway flickered, popped, exploded into and out of existence.

The image settled.

John Murray smiled.

"Okay..." he said. "You ready?"

Ashton looked tense. This was where John Murray would try to have his system take control of the portal on both sides. "Moment of truth, John. I do wish you luck."

"Thank you, Ashton..." John said matter-of-factly. "But you're ready in any case."

Ashton allowed a quick glance at Peter before responding.

"We're ready." Ashton hesitated, then signaled to his assistant, who was patiently standing at the lever he had raised to first engage the gateway.

The assistant lowered the lever.

Other than a slight flickering of electricity along the three bands encircling the portal, there was no change.

"You have 'em both," Ashton told John Murray.

John was carefully monitoring his boards and monitors. Everyone on both sides of the gateway appeared to be holding a collective breath.

John finally gave a cautious nod. "Bridge is holding."

Ashton waited a few more seconds before finally allowing himself a slight smile.

"Fantastic, John."

"Certainly is," said John.

One of the three bands encircling the portal flickered.

"John?" Ashton asked anxiously.

"I'm on it."

Everyone waited. The professor stood stoically in the background. Those gathered around him watched nervously, uncertain as to what was going on.

"John?" Ashton repeated. He placed a hand gently on Peter's shoulder.

"It's the time differential algorithm," said John. "Give me a second."

"You only have a second."

John continued to work frantically at his computer.

The image flickered again.

John Murray looked up at Ashton. He looked calm but crestfallen.

"The time flow on your side isn't static," he explained. "There's no way the algorithm can adapt." He glanced again at one of his monitors, then spoke coolly. "Collapse imminent."

"I understand," said Ashton. "I am really sorry, John."

Ben, standing directly beside Professor LaMothe, had an idea of what this meant. "Professor?"

The professor didn't respond, couldn't look down into the questioning face of the boy.

Ashton spoke evenly. "I'm sending Peter over."

John Murray wouldn't be able to stop the collapse of the bubble, but he wasn't quite finished.

"Not yet!"

"If we don't get him to the other side before the bubble collapses, we're all--"

"I know! I know!"

"Then what--"

"I can still save the children."

"How?"

John Murray was too busy to respond.

Julie moved nearer the professor.

"What does he mean?" she asked.

The professor, after a moment's hesitation, answered without looking away from the portal.

"Peter must be awakened. He must pass through the portal before it closes or those on the dream side will never reintegrate... and we will never wake."

"The children, Professor. What about the children?"

"When the bubble collapses..."

Ben spoke with a sense of finality. "Like the rest of the dream... we will cease to exist."

The professor did not acknowledge the comment. He said nothing further, focused his attention again fully on the gateway and on John Murray, who was hurrying frenziedly about in the laboratory in the real world.

Ashton took a hesitant step nearer the portal, bringing Peter with him.

"John?" he urged anxiously.

"I got it!" John blurted. "I got it! Send him!"

Ashton slid his hand from Peter's shoulder to the middle of his back and pushed him gently but firmly toward the gateway.

Peter looked lost. Stumbling nearer the portal, he turned his head and looked back at Ben and Julie. He became a dark silhouette in front of the bright blue of the gateway.

Ben lifted a hand to bid Peter goodbye, but Peter was already turning his head forward.

Ben lowered his hand back to his side.

Peter stepped through.

"Done!" Ashton called out.

At that moment, the gateway silently shut down.

A heartbeat later, Ashton vanished. There was no sound, no sudden flash. He just wasn't there anymore.

His assistants disappeared.

Professor LaMothe took a deep breath. Ben turned to look up at him, but he wasn't in time. The professor was gone.

The room grew deadly quiet. Not even the sound of the generator in the other room could be heard. Ben looked around them in quiet desperation, eventually faced Julie.

"What do you think is going to happen?" he asked.

There was a very faint whispering noise, as of a light breeze blowing through trees that were still clinging to dry leaves.

The sound grew steadily louder.

"Julie?"

Julie turned slowly about, but could see nothing that would cause the sound. She looked over at Ben and shook her head in answer.

The walls around them slowly faded, turning a misty gray. The mist was emptiness... a void.

The void crept in on them from all directions. As it did, objects dematerialized, faded into nothing.

Julie tried her best to give her brother a comforting smile.

"I guess I'll see ya' later, Ben."

The void enveloped everything.

Chapter Eleven

Adult Ben Foster leaned against the wall beside the front window. He looked calmly out at the neighborhood.

Julie and Louis were sitting on the other side of the living room. Louis was watching Ben, but Julie was looking down, her hands resting in her lap.

Ben let out a half-satisfied sigh. "John Murray had managed to create this... *world*... just in time. He got us out."

"S'pose so," said Julie.

"We're here."

"Yeah..." Julie brought her hands up and folded her arms.

Ben looked questioning at his grown sister. "Yeah..."

Louis didn't like the sound of this. "What's that supposed to mean?" he asked. He didn't direct his question to one or the other. He would accept an answer from either one.

Ben shrugged and turned back to the window.

Julie leaned back in her seat.

Louis was growing perturbed. "Hey. We <u>are</u> here... right?"

"We're here," said Ben.

"Well okay, then."

The three of them grew quiet again. The room, the house, the neighborhood, the world, all fell into a heavy silence. Julie and Louis settled back in the couch. Ben continued to study the scene outside.

When he spoke again, he didn't look back in the room. "I have the weirdest feeling," he said. His words sent barely a ripple through the quiet, and yet there was an ominous quality to the words.

"Yeah, well I was fine until a minute ago," said Louis.

Ben grinned, but continued to look outside. "Sorry," he said apologetically.

The silence closed in again, but Louis wasn't going to let it stay.

"You can't just say something like that and then drop it, Ben."

"It feels like... it's almost as though..." Ben let the sentence fade.

Julie picked up the thought. "As though one second you're in the laboratory, and the next you're here."

Ben stared curiously at Julie, deciphering her words. He struggled with the concept.

"Something like that."

Louis was growing increasingly unsettled, as he often did when around these two. "I don't like where this is going," he mumbled, almost to himself.

Ben was still leaning beside the window, but he was now looking at his companions in the room.

"I feel like I have the history of all these years, but no real memories of them passing."

"Like data," said Julie.

"Like data." Ben visibly struggled with his thoughts for a long time. He finally pushed himself from the wall and stepped directly in front of the window. He stuffed his hands into his pockets. "I know that Mike Margolis fought in some war and became a hero. His brother Tony was a state senator, but had to resign in disgrace. I don't remember why. Donna is working on her third marriage, has four kids, most of 'em grown; named the first one Mike."

Ben looked over his shoulder at Louis. "You're an associate professor," he said, then looked at Julie before turning back to the window. "You're a lawyer for an advocacy group."

"And you're a writer," said Julie. She tried to remember, but... "I have nothing about Peter... he's not here."

"You and I spend all our holidays together," said Ben. "The fact that we never see our parents never seems to come up in conversation."

Louis slid forward and sat on the edge of the couch. "If John Murray created this world for us, why not put our parents in it?"

"He duplicated the world of the dream bubble, including us," said Ben.

"But our parents weren't of the dream bubble," finished Julie. "They were real."

Louis let that settle in for a few seconds before bringing it back around to the larger question.

"Real or not, have we lived our lives all these years or not?"

"I don't think so," Julie said flatly.

"But…"

"John Murray didn't want to abandon the children," said Ben. "Born in the dream bubble or not. He could save us, but then what? A neighborhood of children, suddenly without parents? But what if he could add in an algorithm that could extrapolate out likely events running out from the moment of the bubble's collapse, and create an alternate world set decades later? Children all grown up?"

"He gave us lives lived," said Julie.

"I don't know, man," Louis said, still unsure. "That's way too weird."

"Maybe, but it answers this odd feeling I have," said Ben.

"I agree," said Julie. "But… then… we don't know what we're supposed to feel like. What's normal?'

At the sound of an engine, Ben turned around again to the window. He watched a fifty year old moving van come into Ravenhill Court. It stopped a house or two up from the Foster house.

Julie and Louis came up beside Ben. They watched a middle-aged woman step out of the passenger side. A moment later, a similarly aged man came around from the other side of the vehicle and studied the neighborhood.

"I think that's Mike," said Ben.

"Could be," said Louis.

Julie watched the activity in the street for a few moments, then frowned, crinkled her brows.

"I have a question for you…" she said.

Louis looked at her expectantly. Ben, however, continued to look out the window. He had a hardened expression on his face.

Julie let out a sigh, then another. "What are we doing here?" she finally asked.

"What do you mean?" asked Louis.

"What made you come here, Louis? Today?"

"I…" Louis had no answer.

"And what about Mike? He's moving back? On the same day that we just happen to show up?"

Ben spoke softly but with a calm certainty. "We're all coming back… we're coming home."

An early sixties era car pulled into the driveway of the Osborne home across the street. A grown Donna Osborne climbed out of the passenger, her husband from the driver's side.

Donna looked a bit bewildered.

Julie gently clasped her brother's arm.

Ben, Julie and Louis looked silently out on the neighborhood that would be their home for as long as this virtual world existed.

Julie sensed something in her brother and looked up at him. She saw a warm grin slowly appear on his face.

"What is it?"

Ben tried to dismiss the question, but Julie was intrigued by his growing change of emotion. She leaned in and raised a brow in one her *'come on, give...'* expressions.

"It's nothing, really..." he said. "I was just wondering, you know... what they're doing out in the real world right now. I mean, think about it... what if only a few seconds have passed since they left?"

Unsettled looks spread across the faces of both Julie and Louis.

Ben watched side-glance as Julie slowly tilted her head slightly and glanced upward.

"Helloooo?" she called out softly.

Ben shook his head and grinned openly. "Geez, Julie..."

Louis managed to relax then, and put on a genuine smile of his own.

"Man, this is too weird," he said.

Ben continued to look out on the activity going on in street below them, but couldn't help but glance a bit anxiously up at the evening sky overhead...

end